This book is due for return on or before the last date indicated
on label. Renewals may be obtained on application.

PERTH AND KINROSS DISTRICT LIBRARY

Text copyright © 1989 Jill Paton Walsh
Illustrations copyright © 1989 Alan Marks

First published in Great Britain by
Macdonald Children's Books 1989
Reprinted in 1990 by Simon and Schuster Young Books

Photoset in 16pt Garamond by Goodfellow & Egan
Colour origination by Scantrans Pte Ltd, Singapore

Printed and bound in Belgium by
Proost International Book Production

Simon and Schuster Young Books
Simon and Schuster Ltd
Wolsey House, Wolsey Road
Hemel Hempstead HP2 4SS

British Library Cataloguing in Publication Data
Paton Walsh, Jill *1937–*
   Birdy and the ghosties.
   I. Title II. Marks, Alan
   823'.914[J]

ISBN 0-356-16779-8
ISBN 0-7500-0684-6

Jill Paton Walsh

Birdy *and the* GHOSTIES

Illustrated by Alan Marks

S I M O N   &   S C H U S T E R

LONDON • SYDNEY • NEW YORK • TOKYO • SINGAPORE • TORONTO

692315
JS

For Jessica

Chapter One

There was once a little girl called Bird
Janet, or Birdy for short. She lived with
Papajack, her father, and Mamalucy, her
mother, in a cottage where three things
met. These three things were a road, a
river, and the sea.

Papajack had a stout little boat, called
Grey Goose, and he worked as a
ferryman, rowing people across the river,
and saving them a long walk inland to
the bridge upstream.

Mamalucy baked buttery bannocks on the black range in the cottage kitchen. She could often sell a bannock to one of the travellers on the road, or to someone taking shelter in the cottage porch while they waited for Papajack to come back from the further side, and row them over the river.

Birdy was too little to help much, but she did her best to be useful to her mother, milking the goat when she got up in the morning, and gathering the rough-shelled dark mussels that clung to the rocks on the sea-shore, to help fill the supper pot on the range.

Now, most of the people who came on
the road to the ferryman's cottage
wanted only to be rowed to the other side
of the river, but just now and then
someone came who wanted to be rowed
to the offshore island, where there were a
few wind-swept farms.

Then Papajack had to row across a
mile of rowdy water, where the white
horses gambolled and raced.

When that happened Mamalucy would leave her work, and Birdy would leave her play, and the two together would stand at the cottage window, and watch the ferryboat all the way over and all the way back.

"Aren't you frighted, Papajack," asked Birdy, "riding the bucking water . . . ?"

"No, I'm not frighted, Birdy,"
Papajack told her. "But I am careful. The
sea is full of danger, although it means no
harm. It makes me think what I'm about;
but it doesn't make me tremble as a
robber would, or a ghostie. And it's
daytime work too, when a man can see
everything around him, and reckon
what's what."

9

Chapter Two

It happened one day that a wrinkled old woman came down to the river bank, with holes in her shoes, and she said to Papajack, "I've never a penny to pay you with, my dear, but I must have a ride over the river."

"Well, if you must, you must," said Papajack, for he had a kind heart. "In you get, then."

Now the boat wasn't easy to row with only one passenger in it. Papajack had to sit in the middle, to work the oars, and if there was somebody in the back of the boat, and nobody up in the front, the boat didn't ride level and easy. So Birdy jumped into the boat, and sat right in the front for the ride, and off they went.

The sun was shining, and the water was running clear, and as they went Birdy started to sing a song she knew:

"Grey goose and gander,
Waft your wings together,
Carry the good king's daughter
Over the one strand river!"

And when they got to the other side the old woman got out of the boat, and she said to Papajack, "You want to watch that girl of yours."

"I do watch her," said Papajack. "She's dear as salt to me. But why do you say that?"

"She's got second sight," the old woman said. "And you can't be too careful with second sight. There's no knowing what you'll see!"

"I haven't got second sight!" said Birdy. She didn't like the sound of it, to tell the truth.

"Well, how come that you know who I am, then?" said the old woman. "The good king's daughter, that's me!"

So Papajack and Birdy both gave her a good looking at, what with the holes in her shoes, and the raggedy look of her, and they didn't believe her. But it would have been rude to say so.

"What's the one strand river, then?" said Birdy, instead. "Didn't I ought to know that, if I'm so clever?"

"Everyone crosses it sooner or later," the old woman said. "You're too young to know about it, I expect."

"It's the sea, isn't it?" said Birdy. She didn't like being called too young.

"No it isn't," said the old woman. "The sea's got a second side if you go over it far enough. You'll just have to wait till you're wiser. Give me the bannock you've got hid in your apron pocket now; I'm hungrier than you are!"

So Birdy gave it to her. The old woman set off on her road, and Papajack rowed the boat back over to the cottage side.

"Mad as a bat, that one," he said to Birdy.

"But she might be a king's daughter," said Birdy. "I expect she was a princess once, to her own dear father."

"Don't let her worry you, girl," said Papajack. "Don't you give a second thought to what she said."

But Birdy couldn't help it. She did wonder about second sight. For a day or two she practised looking twice at everything, and it was perfectly true that she noticed more the second time she looked.

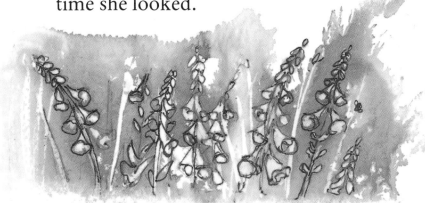

The first time she looked at the foxgloves growing by the gate she saw the speckled flowers; and the second time she looked she saw two or three bees that had crawled right into them.

The first time she looked along the beach she saw a bit of old driftwood; and the second time she looked she saw a fine ship's spar, that would make a good oar for the ferryboat.

The first time she looked at the shore in the morning she saw the waves breaking bright on the pale sand, and the thrift and sea-carrot growing in the cliff-top grasses; the second time she looked she saw it was a fine world to live in.

But she was only a little girl, and she soon forgot about looking twice.

Until the day the ghosties came.

Chapter Three

They came very early in the morning.
Birdy and Papajack and Mamalucy were
still eating their breakfast. There was a
great loud knocking, but when Papajack
opened the door there was nothing
outside except voices.

"Fetch your oars, ferryman, fetch your
oars," said the voices. "We need you to
row us over!"

But there seemed to be nobody there. Only a gruff voice, a soft voice, and a high voice, all saying "Hurry, ferryman, hurry! Get in your boat!"

"I'll just get my coat," says Papajack, "and bring the last bite of my breakfast along with me." For he thought someone was playing a joke on him.

So he got down into his boat, and set the oars ready in the rowlocks. And there was nobody at all in sight.

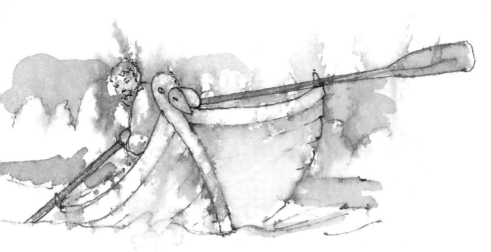

But then suddenly the boat bucked in the quiet water. It dipped and it lurched as if someone had stepped into it, and it tipped down at the back a bit with someone's weight. And then again another no one got into it, and rocked it for a moment and weighed it down more. Then lastly someone little and nifty got in, and moved from side to side looking for a place to settle, and then sat down in the middle. And the boat was tipped up so that the back was almost under the water, and the front was rearing up high.

"We can't go nowhere like this," said
Papajack. "What you've put in the boat
is too heavy."

"You must put your daughter up in the
front," said the gruff voice, "to even us
out."

"Well, she don't weigh much more than
a pigeon," said Papajack. "She'll never
do it."

But when Birdy, who had been
listening at the cottage door, ran and got
into the front of the boat,
sitting up in the
prow at her father's
back, the boat
straightened up
at once, and rode
level in the water.

"I've heard about this, Birdy," said Papajack, "but I never expected it to happen. And we'd much better not offend them." And then he asked the invisible voices, "Where are we going, then? Is it over the river?"

"Oh, no!" said the voices. "Row us far out, far out. Out to the second island."

"You must be strangers in these parts," said Papajack. "There's only one island out there."

"You haven't looked this morning, ferryman," said the soft voice. "Look again."

So both Birdy and Papajack looked out to sea, and there they saw a second island, where there had never ever been more than one before.

It was a blue, blue shadow on the
horizon, where the sea and the sky met.
And it looked like a fine large island, but
it certainly hadn't been there yesterday,
or the day before yesterday, or any other
day they remembered.

"So its taking nobody nowhere, is it?"
said Papajack. "Well, sooner we go
sooner we'll be home again . . ." and
he pulled hard on the oars and they
were off.

Chapter Four

At first the flow of the river helped them,
taking them quickly out to sea. The sea
was still golden in the morning light, and
the waves were breaking white all over it.
But where the ferryboat went, a path of
smoothness stretched out in front of it
and behind, and Papajack rowed in a
dead calm, on a ribbon of water as flat
and quiet as glass.

Birdy could see the little fishes swimming a fathom down, and the sea birds came in flocks and landed in the boat's wake as though it had been sheltered water.

All the way to the sudden island the sea-road shone ahead of them.

"Are you all right, Papajack?" asked Birdy, half-way over. "It's a long, long way to row."

"The rowing's all right," said Papajack. "But I wish I could see my passengers. It worries me not knowing what's in the boat with me!"

So Birdy stood up in the prow, so that she could see over her father's shoulders, and she looked at the back of the boat. She looked once, and she saw the boat clear empty; the bench with nothing on it but scratched paint and bright drops of salt water.

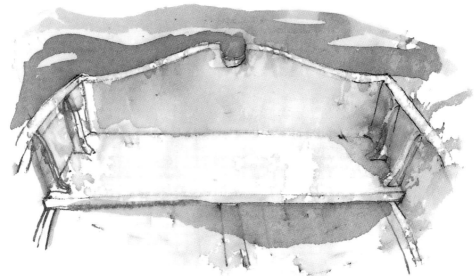

Then she looked twice, and she saw
three horrible ghosties sitting there, riding
in the boat with them, face to face.

There was a craggy great man ghostie,
with crevices of slime in his flesh, covered
in sea-valves and clothed in rotting
strands of weed. And beside him sat a
woman ghostie hinged and scaled like a
crawfish, with dozens of tentacles,
waving. And between them sat a child
ghostie, covered in greasy black feathers
like a cormorant, and clutching a
bleeding and rotting fish in its claws.

Birdy drew in her breath. And even over the sound of the white waves dancing and breaking to the left and to

the right of them, Papajack heard his daughter sigh.

"What can you see, Birdy?" he said.

But Birdy thought twice before telling.

She remembered Papajack saying the sea didn't scare him as much as a ghostie would; and he was sitting even closer than she was . . .

So she said, "Oh, Papajack, dear father, there's a king and a queen and a prince with us! There's a king with a wise face, and a bright crown, wrapped up in a cloak of sea-blue; and a queen with a kind face, and sun-gold, sand-gold hair, wearing a dress of sea-green; and their child is a boy of about my age, with black, black, hair, and he's sitting between them, smiling."

"Oh well, that's a relief then," said Papajack. "That's much better news than I feared. And it must be only the gold that they're wearing that makes them so deathly heavy to row! How much further, Birdy, to go?"

Birdy looked at the shadow island, and saw it was near now, looming up between them and the sun, and casting a darkness over the water towards them. "Not far now," she said.

And she looked again at the back of the boat. She looked once, and she saw the terrible ghosties, so that the sight of them trembled her bones, and sent shivers running up her back.

She looked twice, and she saw a king and a queen and a prince sitting there, wearing sea-blue, and sea-green, and all smiling at her, bright and kindly. And in the prince's arms was a cradle-toy loved into a strange shape, like her own felt rabbit, her bedtime comforter.

"Well, what's true?" said Birdy, full of amazement.

"We get stuck with how people see us," said the ghostie king. "And some people do have the horrors! What we were just now is what we got for getting stuck in a trawl net and scaring a fisherman a hundred years back. You're a brave girl, and very good-hearted to see us so kindly."

And the ghost boy began jumping about, rocking the boat and shouting, "Ma! Da! Look at me, look at me! Doesn't she think I'm handsome!"

"Sit down, Mumpsimus," said the ghostie king, "you're rocking the boat."

"Well, what's her reward going to be?" said the ghostie boy. "We've got to give her something. Story kings are always giving prizes."

"Get out of the boat with us now, and any of the farms on the island is yours for ever," said the ghostie king, waving his hand.

Chapter Five

By now they had come quite close to the beach of the strange new island. And Birdy saw the island in front of her, rising gently from a circle of golden sands. She saw a land softly folded in sheltered valleys. There were silver streams and bright green meadows, and masses of almond trees all in pink flower, and cottages built of rosy stone, with walled-round gardens, and a little town beyond a harbour, where she could see people walking and talking together –

only there was no church, neither tower nor spire nor bell.

So Birdy looked twice, and she saw no island at all, nothing but a scattered skerry, a stack of black rocks covered only with seaweed that fidgeted around in the shifting water like grass in the wind. There were a few glum sea-birds standing on the wave-washed crags, and that was all.

"We don't want a farm here, thank you," she said. "I think we'll go home to Mother."

"But we've got to give her something," said Mumpsimus.

"Certainly we'll give her something," said the ghostie queen. "What do you want, Birdy?"

"Careful, now, girl," said Papajack.

"Can you take away the second sight?" said Birdy. "I'd rather have second thoughts, any time. I see that the world's what we make of it. But I don't like the jumping about and the scary surprises."

"No, I can't," said the ghost queen. "Or I won't, rather. If you've got that, you've got it. If you've had it you wouldn't like losing it. Like it or lump it, so you might as well like it."

"I'm glad you've got it," said the ghostie boy. "You got rid of those black greasy feathers for me."

He smiled at Birdy, and he said to her, "It'll have to be this, then," and he gave her his cradle-toy, and a funny-shaped bundle it was, too.

And then suddenly the boat was lightened, and lightened again, and lightened a third time, and Birdy in the prow was weighting it nose-down, so she had to move herself quickly.

"They've gone, then," said Papajack.

Birdy looked hard at the skerries, and there were three grey-green seals lolling on a crop of rock. She didn't look at them twice. The boat pulled away from them, as Papajack began the long row home.

Chapter Six

"He gave me a present," she said, half-way back.

"For what it's worth," said Papajack.

And Birdy saw that the ghostie cradle-toy was only a bundle of a torn fishing net, full of mussel shells.

"It's a supper," she said. "Without my having to gather them."

"There is that," said Papajack, "and us home in safety, and hungry."

And then, when Mamalucy opened the mussels for supper there was a huge great pearl in every one.

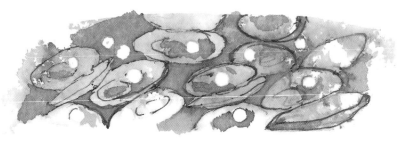

Papajack looked at the pearls piled up shining and sheeny on the kitchen table, and he saw the wages of a strong young lad to help him. And

Mamalucy looked at the pearls, and she saw the cottage white-washed, and a dresser with blue and white plates on it standing in the kitchen, and a shell-pink wedding dress for Birdy, one day someday . . .

"To think this could happen to everyday people like us!" she said. "As long as I live I'll never get over it!"

"That's it!" cried Birdy, suddenly remembering what the old woman said to her, and the puzzling words in the song.

"*That's* what the one strand river is – the one strand river is something you remember for ever – the one strand river is whatever you never get over."

And Birdy looked at the heap of pearls, gleaming like sunlit rain-clouds, and she saw the ghost boy's friendship, that she would never, ever get over, and she smiled.

WITHDRAWN

PRINTED IN BELGIUM BY

proost
INTERNATIONAL BOOK PRODUCTION